FEVER DREAM
NIGHT
LIGHTS

FEVER DREAM

ILLUSTRATED BY

DARREL ANDERSON

NIGHT LIGHTS

RAY BRADBURY

St. Martin's Press/New York

Published by St. Martin's Press
175 Fifth Avenue, New York, New York 10010.

The NIGHT LIGHTS series is produced by Armadillo Press.

Library of Congress Cataloging-in-Publication Data

Bradbury, Ray, 1920—
Fever dream.

(Night lights series)
Summary: A young boy's illness comes alive taking over his body bit by bit until he dies—but the virus remains alive in his body.
[1. Horror stories] I. Title. II. Series.
PZ7.B717Fe 1986 [Fic] 86-33867
ISBN 0-312-57285-9

Book design and original NIGHT LIGHTS concept by:
Dave Orlon
Production: Richard Salvucci

Typesetting: Robert K. Wiener/ARCHITYPE
Special thanks to Carol and Steven, Parkinson International.

Manufactured in South Korea

FEVER DREAM

They put him between fresh, clean, laundered sheets, and there was always a newly squeezed glass of thick orange juice on the table under the dim, pink lamp. All Charles had to do was call, and Mom or Dad would stick their heads into his room to see how sick he was. The acoustics of the room were fine; you could hear the toilet gargling its porcelain throat of mornings, you could hear rain tap the roof or sly mice run in the secret walls or the canary singing in its cage downstairs. If you were very alert, sickness wasn't too bad.

He was thirteen, Charles was. It was mid-September, with the land beginning to burn with autumn. He lay in the bed for three days before the terror overcame him.

His hand began to change. His right hand. He looked at it, and it was hot and sweating there on the counterpane alone. It fluttered, it moved a bit. Then it lay there, changing color.

That afternoon the doctor came again and tapped his thin chest like a little drum. "How are you?" asked the doctor, smiling. "I know, don't tell me: 'My *cold* is fine, Doctor, but *I* feel awful!' Ha!" He laughed at his own oft-repeated joke.

Charles lay there, and for him that terrible and ancient jest was becoming a reality. The joke fixed itself in his mind. His mind touched and drew away from it in a pale terror. The doctor did not know how cruel he was with his jokes!

"Doctor," whispered Charles, lying flat and colorless. "My *hand*, it doesn't *belong* to me anymore. This morning it *changed* into something else. I want you to change it back, Doctor, Doctor!"

The doctor showed his teeth and patted his hand. "It looks fine to me, son. You just had a little fever dream."

"But it changed, Doctor, oh, Doctor," cried Charles, pitifully holding up his pale, wild hand. "It *did!*"

The doctor winked. "I'll give you a pink pill for that." He popped a tablet onto Charles's tongue. "Swallow!"

"Will it make my hand change back and become *me* again?"

"Yes, yes."

The house was silent when the doctor drove off down the road in his car under the quiet blue September sky. A clock ticked far below in the kitchen world. Charles lay looking at his hand.

It did not change back. It was still something else.

The wind blew outside. Leaves fell against the cool window.

At four o'clock his other hand changed. It seemed almost to become a fever. It pulsed and shifted, cell by cell. It beat like a warm heart. The fingernails turned blue and then red. It took about an hour for it to change, and when it was finished, it looked just like any ordinary hand. But it was not ordinary. It no longer was him anymore. He lay in a fascinated horror and then fell into an exhausted sleep.

Mother brought the soup up at six. He wouldn't touch it. "I haven't any hands," he said, eyes shut.

"Your hands are perfectly good," said Mother.

"No," he wailed. "My hands are gone. I feel like I have stumps. Oh. Mama, Mama, hold me, hold me, I'm scared!"

She had to feed him herself.

"Mama," he said, "get the doctor, please, again. I'm so sick."

"The doctor'll be here tonight at eight,"she said, and went out.

At seven, with night dark and close around the house, Charles was sitting up in bed when he felt the thing happening to first one leg and then the other. "Mama!

Come quick!" he screamed.

But when Mama came, the thing was no longer happening. When she went downstairs, he simply lay without fighting as his legs beat and beat, grew warm, red-hot, and the room filled with the warmth of his feverish change. The glow crept up from his toes to his ankles and then to his knees.

"May I come in?" The doctor smiled in the doorway.

"Doctor!" cried Charles. "Hurry, take off my blankets!"

The doctor lifted the blankets tolerantly. "There you are. Whole and healthy. Sweating, though. A little fever. I told you not to move around, bad boy."

He pinched the moist, pink cheek. "Did the pills help? Did your hand change back?"

"No, no, now it's my other hand and my legs!"

"Well, well, I'll have to give you three more pills, one

for each limb, eh, my little peach?" laughed the doctor.

"Will they help me? Please, please. What've I *got?*"

"A mild case of scarlet fever, complicated by a slight cold."

"Is it a germ that lives and has more little germs in me?"

"Yes."

"Are you *sure* it's scarlet fever? You haven't taken any tests!"

"I guess I know a certain fever when I see one," said the doctor, checking the boy's pulse with cool authority.

Charles lay there, not speaking until the doctor was crisply packing his black kit. Then, in the silent room, the boy's voice made a small, weak pattern, his eyes alight with remembrance. "I read a book once. About petrified trees, wood turning to stone. About how trees fell and rotted and minerals got in and built up and they look just like trees, but they're not, they're stone." He stopped. In the quiet, warm room his breathing sounded.

"Well?" asked the doctor.

"I've been thinking," said Charles after a time. "Do germs ever get big? I mean, in biology class they told us about one-celled animals, amoebas and things, and how millions of years ago they got together until there was a bunch and they made the first body. And more and more cells got together and got bigger and then finally maybe there was a fish and finally here *we* are, and all we are is a bunch of cells that decided to get together, to help each other out. Isn't that right?" Charles wet his feverish lips.

"What's all this about?" The doctor bent over him.

"I've got to tell you this. Doctor, oh, I've got to!" he cried. "What would happen, oh just pretend, please

At nine o'clock the doctor was escorted out to his car by the mother and father, who handed him his bag. They conversed in the cool night wind for a few minutes. "Just be sure his hands are kept strapped to his legs," said the doctor. "I don't want him hurting himself."

"Will he be all right, Doctor?" The mother held to his arm a moment.

He patted her shoulder. "Haven't I been your family physician for thirty years? It's the fever. He imagines things."

"But those bruises on his throat, he almost choked himself."

"Just you keep him strapped; he'll be all right in the morning."

The car moved off down the dark September road.

At three in the morning Charles was still awake in his small, black room. The bed was damp under his head and his back. He was very warm. Now he no longer had any arms or legs, and his body was beginning to change. He did not move on the bed, but looked at the vast, blank ceiling space with insane concentration. For a while he had screamed and thrashed, but now he was weak and hoarse from it, and his mother had gotten up a number of times to soothe his brow with a wet towel. Now he was silent, his hands strapped to his legs.

He felt the walls of his body change, the organs shift, the lungs catch fire like burning bellows of pink alcohol. The room was lighted up as with the flickerings of a hearth.

Now he had no body. It was all gone. It was under him, but it was filled with a vast pulse of some burning, lethargic drug. It was as if a guillotine had neatly lopped

off his head, and his head lay shining on a midnight pillow, while the body, below, still alive, belonged to somebody else. The disease had eaten his body and from the eating had reproduced itself in feverish duplicate.

There were the little hand hairs and the fingernails and the scars and the toenails and the tiny mole on his right hip, all done again in perfect fashion.

I am dead, he thought. I've been killed, and yet I live. My body is dead; it is all disease and nobody will know. I will walk around and it will not be me, it will be something else. It will be something all bad, all evil, so big and so evil it's hard to understand or think about. Something that will buy shoes and drink water and get married some day maybe and do more evil in the world than has ever been done. Now the warmth was stealing up his neck, into his cheeks, like a hot wine. His lips burned, his eyelids, like leaves, caught fire. His nostrils breathed out blue flame, faintly, faintly.

This will be all, he thought. It'll take my head and my brain and fix each eye and every tooth and all the marks in my brain, and every hair and every wrinkle in my ears, and there'll be nothing left of me.

He felt his brain fill with a boiling mercury. He felt his left eye clench in upon itself and, like a snail, withdraw, shift. He was blind in his left eye. It no longer belonged to him. It was enemy territory. His tongue was gone, cut out. His left cheek was numbed, lost. His left ear stopped hearing. It belonged to someone else now. This thing that was being born, this mineral thing replacing the wooden log, this disease replacing healthy animal cell.

He tried to scream, and he was able to scream loud and high sharply in the room, just as his brain flooded down, his right eye and right ear were cut out, he was blind and

deaf, all fire, all terror, all panic, all death.

His scream stopped before his mother ran through the door to his side.

It was a good, clear morning, with a brisk wind that helped carry the doctor up the path before the house. In the window above, the boy stood, fully dressed. He did not wave when the doctor waved and called, "What's this? Up? My God!"

The doctor almost ran upstairs. He came gasping into the bedroom.

"What are you doing out of bed?" he demanded of the boy. He tapped his thin chest, took his pulse and temperature. "Absolutely amazing! Normal. Normal, by God!"

"I shall never be sick again in my life," declared the boy quietly, standing there looking out the wide win-

dow. "Never."

"I hope not. Why, you're looking fine, Charles."

"Doctor?"

"Yes, Charles?"

"Can I go to school *now?*" asked Charles.

"Tomorrow will be time enough. You sound positively eager."

"I am. I like school. All the kids. I want to play with them and wrestle with them, and spit on them and play with the girls' pigtails and shake the teacher's hand, and rub my hands on all the cloaks in the cloakroom, and I want to grow up and travel and shake hands with people all over the world, and be married and have lots of children, and go to libraries and handle books and—*all* of that, I want to!" said the boy, looking off into the September morning. "What's the name you called me?"

"What?" The doctor puzzled. "I called you nothing

but Charles."

"It's better than no name at all, I guess." The boy shrugged.

"I'm glad you want to go back to school," said the doctor.

"I really anticipate it," smiled the boy. "Thank you for your help, Doctor. Shake hands."

"Glad to."

They shook hands gravely, and the clear wind blew through the open window. They shook hands for almost a minute, the boy smiling up at the old man and thanking him.

Then, laughing, the boy raced the doctor downstairs and out to his car. His mother and father followed for the happy farewell.

"Fit as a fiddle!" said the doctor. "Incredible!"

"And strong," said the father. "He got out of his

straps himself during the night. Didn't you, Charles?"

"Did I?" said the boy.

"You did! How?"

"Oh," the boy said, "that was a long time ago."

"A long time ago!"

They all laughed, and while they were laughing the quiet boy moved his bare foot on the sidewalk and merely touched, brushed, against a number of red ants that were scurrying about on the sidewalk. Secretly, his eyes shining while his parents chatted with the old man, he saw the ants hesitate, quiver, and lie still on the cement. He sensed they were cold now.

"Good-bye!"

The doctor drove away, waving.

The boy walked ahead of his parents. As he walked he looked away toward the town and began to hum

"School Days" under his breath.

"It's good to have him well again," said the father.

"Listen to him. He's so looking forward to school!"

The boy turned quietly. He gave each of his parents a crushing hug. He kissed them both several times.

Then without a word he bounded up the steps into the house.

In the parlor, before the others entered, he quickly opened the bird cage, thrust his hand in, and petted the yellow canary, once.

Then he shut the cage door, stood back, and waited.